TRULY ERASED

Written by Lynn Arren

* All characters and events in this book are fiction and come from the imagination of Lynn Arren. Any resemblances to actual persons or events are completely coincidental.

Chapter 1: The Search Continues

"Claire..." my father gently pushed my bedroom door open. He stood in his robe and slippers, rubbing his eyes. "You have school tomorrow. Don't you think you should go to bed?"

I looked at the time on my computer screen. It was 2:02 AM. I actually had school *today*. But I couldn't stop now. I didn't care about sleep. I only cared about researching until I knew how to break Benjamin free from the dreadful curse that controlled his life and made him miserable.

"I'm working on an assignment," I lied. "It's due tomorrow... I've been procrastinating."

"Well, I hope you're learning an important lesson. It's best to just sit down and get the work done, and then be done with it. Then you don't have to stay up all hours of the night and you can get yourself a good night's sleep," He told me.

"Yeah, Dad. I am," I told him. He slowly closed my door as he left my room. I felt bad lying to my dad, but I didn't lie about everything. I was, in fact, learning a lesson. The lesson was that I, Claire Elizabeth Walker, was totally unable to give up on a future with Benjamin. I loved him, and I would do anything to be with him. Even if that meant spending every single night on the computer, researching anything and everything I could find that might help me discover a way to break the curse.

It had only been three weeks since Benjamin had left me (again, for the second time). The thought sent jolts of pain through my heart, but I wouldn't let it depress me this time. I was determined. I knew I had one more week before the next full moon, and I was going to have a plan by then if it was the last thing I did.

Jacquelyn thought I was absolutely insane. I didn't really blame her. She'd always tell me she knows I love him, but the fact that Benjamin had left me not once - but *twice* - was pretty solid proof that he didn't love me in return. But I knew she was wrong.

In fact, Benjamin loved me so much; that's *why* he left me. He wanted me to have a life outside of that stupid ship. The problem was that I didn't want a life that didn't include him. The only solution was to break the curse, and then Benjamin could have a life with me on the shore. That's the only way we could be happy together. And I was determined to make that a reality.

Of course, we already knew how to break the curse. My ancestor was actually the one who placed it on The Serpent's Skull - Benjamin's ship. She intended for Benjamin's father (who was *not* a good man) to be cursed forever. But unfortunately, when Benjamin's father died, the curse was passed on to him, as he was the new Captain of the ship. *Thy shall lose thy love by thy own hand*, that's how the curse can be broken. Benjamin would have to kill the woman he loved.

As fate and the crazy karmic powers in our universe would have it, the woman that Benjamin loved was me. And he refused to end my life (thank God). So here I was, trying to find a new way. There just *had* to be a different way.

I continued searching online. There were hundreds of advertisements to buy books about pirates and witches, but I had a feeling none of them would hold the answer that I longed for. Eventually, my eyelids won the battle they'd been fighting and I passed out on my laptop.

Chapter 2: Sleep Is Overrated

"Are you alright?" Jacquelyn approached my locker from the left. She startled me, and I jumped. Then, I yawned.

"Yeah.. I'm just tired," I told her.

"I see that, Claire. You look like a freaking zombie!" she shouted. "You need to sleep. Why don't you skip last period and head home to your bed?"

It was very unlike Jacquelyn to encourage skipping class. She was our valedictorian, after all. School and academics were always her number one priority.

"I'm fine. I'm going to grab an energy drink," I said. She was right. I did need to sleep. But, I also needed to graduate and get out of Trenton High if I was ever going to have a future with Benjamin.

"Those are horrible for you!" She scolded. I laughed. She was right about that, too. We read all about some of the dangerous chemicals in many of them in health class. But I figured one energy drink wouldn't hurt me too much.

"Well, I have a test next period and I can't skip it. I *need* to graduate," I told her. It was true. Graduation was a week away, and I needed to make sure I passed all of my final exams. I had to graduate and get out of that place. Highschool just didn't do it for me - I wanted to see the world, with Benjamin, preferably.

"Okay, Claire," Jacquelyn started. I knew her tone. I knew what was coming. I sighed. "I'm starting to get really worried about you. Even more worried than I'd been before," she said.

I slammed my locker shut. "Jacquelyn, there's nothing to be worried about. I didn't sleep well last night. I'm going to go to bed early tonight to make up for it."

"You've been this way since we got back," she insisted. It was true. I'd spent every spare minute, including my sleeping hours, researching a way to break the curse. I hadn't slept at all the past three weeks.

As Jacquelyn walked me to my last class, we passed David and Jon's lockers. Both boys hadn't been back to school since we returned to Trenton. I heard their parents had pulled them out to finish up the last few weeks of highschool with private homeschooling tutors. Personally, I think they told their parents that they'd been kidnapped and held hostage by pirates from the 1800s and that their parents sent them to some sort of mental hospital. Or maybe they weren't in an institution, but their parents just didn't want the other kids here to think that they were crazy, so they kept them home. Either way, I had no proof. I only heard rumors about homeschooling. I hadn't seen either one of them out and about in town, either.

Jacquelyn and I decided we'd say we took a little vacation. Of course, our parents were furious. And Camden didn't believe us. But, we were gone a month this time and returned happy and tan (I faked a smile for a while, and our sunburns really did turn to tans eventually!). My therapist said she understood, after the trauma that we'd been through earlier in the year, why we would want to take a vacation to get away from it all. She did scold us for not telling our parents, of course.

My dad grounded me for the whole summer. Jacquelyn's parents did the same. I wasn't allowed to go anywhere but school. He said he couldn't believe that I would put him through that again. He said having one of your children missing is the worst thing anyone could ever experience, and that he's had to do it three times already - all in the same year! I did feel bad for my dad. First, he had to deal with my mother passing away. Then, Camden disappeared. Shortly after, I disappeared. And then I disappeared again. Maybe my dad should be the one seeing a weekly therapist.

I could barely keep my eyes open in my Economics class. I finished my exam and handed it in, yawning three times as I walked my paper to my teacher's desk. I did need to sleep. Unfortunately, I couldn't. Not until I found a way to break the curse and be with Benjamin forever.

Chapter 3: The Lightbulb Goes Off (Finally!)

As soon as I got home, I threw my backpack on my bed and opened up my laptop. The tabs were still up from last night/early this morning.I clicked through to jolt my memory. I scoffed when I couldn't find anything useful.

"Claire?" Camden called from the hallway. He pushed my door open a bit. "Are you hungry?"

Camden was so thoughtful.

"No, I'm good right now. Thanks, though!" I told him. Actually, I was starving. I put my hand on my belly and felt it rumble. I refused to stop searching until I found what I was looking for.

"What are you looking for?" he asked, looking at the screen on my laptop. It was as if he could read my mind.

What exactly was I looking for? I thought about that for a moment. I only knew that I was determined to break the curse that plagued Benjamin, the man I loved. I backed away from the computer. Maybe that was the problem? I didn't know what to look for - I was just aimlessly searching. I'd googled pirates, witches, and curses. I guess I hoped Benjamin's curse would be on a list of curses that were common for pirates and next to it would be an explanation of exactly how to end it. Of course, that never happened.

"I'm not sure," I said slowly. It was true. I realized I needed guidance. I needed someone to point me in the right direction; to give me the name of a book or a specific website. I closed my laptop and changed my mind about eating - I was starving and needed some energy. Plus, I felt like my mind needed a break. I followed

Camden to the kitchen and made myself a peanut butter and jelly sandwich.

As I ate, I thought about how I was going to get some direction. I started to feel a little hopeless, but I quickly shook the feeling away. I would not lose hope. I would figure this out. I was determined.

As I finished the last bite of my sandwich, I pulled out a notebook from the kitchen drawer. I grabbed a pencil and started writing down a few things. I tried to think of words and phrases that were related to my situation. I hoped reading the information would spark a new idea; a new direction to take.

pirates
1800s
witches
curses

I looked over my list, not knowing what good it would even do me. They were just words that had to do with Benjamin's curse. And yet, I felt like maybe I was headed in the right direction…

I continued to write whatever words popped into my head.

time loop

Time loop… I pondered. *1800s…* Suddenly, it was as if the fog was lifted and I was able to clearly make the connection…

"I have to travel back in time!" I shouted aloud. Camden looked at me like I had three heads. I felt my cheeks flush slightly from embarrassment, but didn't let it bother me too much. I'd just realized a way to break the curse. I would have to travel back in time!

Now, I know that sounds absolutely insane. Any normal person would think so. However, I'd been kidnapped twice by pirates from the 1800s who were stuck in a time loop. I was less than a foot away from a witch who actually showed me the past - she allowed me to see and feel what my ancestor was experiencing. So I knew time travel was possible. I didn't know how, but I knew it was possible. If I could travel back in time, I could prevent Arabelle from putting the curse on Stanton. Then, there'd be no curse! I thought about what could go wrong with this new plan of mine. I realized it would be really difficult. First off, I'd have to figure out a way to time travel. Then, I'd have to get myself to the exact location where Arabelle first put the curse on Stanton. I'd have to somehow prevent her from doing that… would she believe me if I told her I was her descendent from the future? Maybe. Maybe not. It didn't matter. I had a plan now, and I was determined to follow it through.

I grabbed a bottle of water from the fridge and ran back to my bedroom. *Finally*, I thought. I *know what to look for*. I quickly typed "ways to travel back in time" in my search bar. A host of websites popped up. Some were selling books, some had stories of people who swear they'd travelled back in time. There were some very scientific sites written by astrophysicists who talked about the possibility of time travel. I didn't even bother to read them. I knew it was real and it was possible - Benjamin was living proof. I just had to figure out how to do it.

Chapter 4: I Couldn't Help Myself

Now that I had a plan, I really got to work. I spent all night researching stories about time travel, time loops, and wormholes. Wormholes were a theoretical phenomenon involving two points that connect two different times in space. It was all very scientific, a lot of it speculative, and some downright bizarre. But I could feel it in my soul that there was some truth to it. After all, there had to be. I knew for a fact that Benjamin was not from the same time or place that I was from. He wore different clothes; he spoke differently. He definitely was trapped in a time loop. And I knew that the full moon had something to do with it, I just didn't know how.

I took a deep breath. What was I to do with all of this information? Yes, I had the startings of a plan. But I had no way to put it into action. Even if I decided to travel back in time right now, I had no idea how to do it. I was going to need help.

That's when I remembered seeing a sign for a palm reader on the boardwalk. Jacquelyn and I had been walking through our ocean-front town a few years back, taking some time to visit the many different gift shops. I spotted the sign and thought it was bizarre; I'd never heard of a palm reader in Trenton. I thought they only existed in the movies. 'Get your palm read here' - that's what the sign read. It was an old sign; I wondered if she was even still in business. I never saw anybody go there. But, I had to try. I didn't like the ideas of witches, gypsies, and palm readers. They spooked me. But especially after my experience with Genevieve, I felt like they might know more than we give them credit for.

I grabbed my backpack and headed out the door.

It was about a fifteen minute walk to the small, broken down shack with the palm reader sign. I heard windchimes, but nothing else. The place looked dead; completely empty. I figured I'd knock on the door just to be sure, but I was fairly certain nobody would answer.

Tap, tap, tap. The door moved wildly as I knocked as gently as possible. It felt like it would break in two at any moment.

"Yes..." I heard an old, screechy voice from the other side. It scared the crap out of me. I instantly had flashbacks to my time with Genevieve and quickly decided that this was a horrible idea. *Never mess with these kinds of people!*, my brain started screaming at me.

Just as I turned to run away, the door swung open. I turned to see who waited there. It was an older woman; chubby, with grey hair tied into a high bun on her head.

"Can I help you?" she asked, in her screechy voice. She sounded like she smoked ten packs of cigarettes a day.

"Oh, um..." I started. Again with the stuttering - it never fails when I'm immensely nervous. "I, uh, I saw your sign." I waited.

"Would you like your palm read, dear?" she asked.

"Um..." I thought for a second. I didn't really want my palm to be read. I was hoping she'd possess some secret wisdom about curses and possibly even time travel. But should I pretend that I was interested in having my palm read so that she'd let me in? I was getting so good at lying lately it was scary.

"Yes, please!" I tried to say enthusiastically. She smiled and held the door open for me, motioning me to enter. I took a breath. I was scared, but I knew I had to be brave. I said a silent prayer to God to protect me, like I'd learned at Sunday school a decade ago. And then I followed the palm reader inside.

Inside the shack was mostly empty. There was no furniture except one small round table and two chairs, opposite one another. On top of the table was a large crystal ball. I couldn't help but giggle to myself.

"Come dear, sit down," the old woman instructed, pointing to one of the chairs. I set my backpack down on the rickety floorboards and sat in the chair.

The old woman walked to the other chair and sat. Her eyes looked me over curiously as she motioned for my hand. I reached over to allow her to hold it.

"Have you had your palm read before?" she asked, staring at its lines. She traced a few of them with her fingertip.

"No," I said. It was true. I'd had a witch tell me all about my past when I was kidnapped by a pirate from the 1800s and stuck on a ship in a time loop, but she hadn't read my palm. I smiled to myself, thinking of how insane that would sound if I said it aloud.

"Well, you have an interesting future," she replied calmly.

I waited for her to continue.

"I see here that your life line breaks in two. That usually means you're going to have a difficult choice to make," she said.

"What kind of a choice?" I asked. It was scary that I was giving this any credibility at all.

"I can't see that. I only see the fork, which splits the line in two. If you make one choice, your life continues on this line..." she showed me on my palm. "And if you make the other choice, your life moves to this line."

I looked at my palm. I could see the line she was talking about. I could see where it split. I still thought it was all a bit silly. I decided it was now or never; time for me to start asking questions to see if this crazy old woman could help me.

"Do you get a lot of customers?" I asked. I doubted it. I hadn't even known for sure if she was still in business when I decided to go there.

"My regulars," she said. "More so when the moon is full." She looked up. I saw stars and a moon glued or nailed to the ceiling.

"They come on the full moon?" I asked, intrigued. That's when Benjamin's ship docked. I wondered, probably foolishly, if any of the pirates from his ship came to her.

"Do you see any pirates?" I blurted out. I couldn't believe I'd just asked that! She would either think I was the most enlightened human, or the stupidest.

She let go of my hand and her stare turned icy.

"That's all for today," she said. "No charge. Come again."

I sat there, confused.

"But you didn't finish..." I started.

"That's all I have for you," she practically yelled, in an angry tone. But I knew that tone. She was afraid. Afraid that if she told me something, somebody would be upset with her. And I knew who - pirates.

I decided to try to be honest with this woman. She was my last hope; the only plan I had. There was no Plan B or C. This was it. I had to do everything in my power to make it work. And then, if it didn't work, well, at least I knew I'd tried my very best.

"I know about the pirates that dock on the full moon," I said softly.

She stared at me, silent.

"They actually kidnapped me - twice," I told her.

She didn't seem surprised.

"I was kind of hoping that you might be able to help me with something related to them.." I started.

"I cannot," she answered swiftly.

"Well, it's not specifically related to them," I said. "It's more related to time travelling." I waited and watched her expression.

"The present moment is a gift. Trust me. You do not want to time travel," she said. I noticed that she didn't discount it or say that it was impossible. Her response gave me hope.

"I know it is. The thing is.. When I was kidnapped, I accidentally fell in love with one of the pirates. But he has this horrible curse on him and he's stuck in a time loop. If I can travel back in time, and stop the curse from ever happening, I could help him. We could be together," I told her honestly.

"You're a stupid girl," she answered after a moment. But then, she sat back down in her chair. "Who would be stupid enough to fall in love with a pirate?"

I laughed. She was right. But I couldn't help myself; it was basically in my DNA. If only she knew I fell in love with the pirate whose sole mission is to end my life and free himself, she'd really think I was stupid.

"I couldn't help it," I said honestly. "It was fate." And that was the truth.

Chapter 5: A Warning

I sat across from the palm reader for about an hour. She told me what she knew about time travel. She said it was possible (as I knew), but very dangerous (as I assumed).

"And visiting the past is one thing..." she said cautiously, "but if you change even one small thing, you change everything." It was a warning, and it made sense. "So if you feel you must go, go, but realize that you hold so many possibilities in your hand based on anything you say or do. Good things, bad things, all things - they can happen because of you." Talk about a lot of pressure.

The palm reader said that she believed in wormholes, and that she believed the pirates we both spoke of were stuck in one and unable to come out the other end. It was hard for my brain to process. She said that magic, time, and space were all heightened during the full moon, and that during a full moon was my best bet to find one. Though she didn't know for sure where any were, she'd had many clients who told her they'd travelled through time. She'd found them peculiar, and even followed one for a bit after completing his palm reading. She said he simply walked off a dock about a half mile away, and instead of falling into the water below, he disappeared into thin air. She said she'd always wondered if he'd gone through a wormhole.

I asked for the exact location of the incident. She told me, and warned me again.

"You think you're helping, but you might make things more miserable - for both of you," she cautioned. "The Universe has a way of ironing out all the wrinkles we create as we go."

I smiled and thanked her for her time. She told me to come back again for a full palm reading, and she didn't even charge me for today's visit.

I quickly grabbed my backpack off the dirty floor and headed to the place on the dock she described a half mile away where her client had disappeared.

I practically ran the whole way; I was just so excited to finally have an action plan.

When I got to the dock, I threw my backpack down on the nearby grass and headed to the end. I took a deep breath. I thought about where I wanted to go: back to the moment before Arabelle put the curse on Stanton's ship. Should I say that out loud? I didn't know how any of this worked. I figured it was worth a shot.

"I want to go back to a few minutes before my ancestor Arabelle put the curse on Stanton's ship," I said out loud, to absolutely nobody. And then I closed my eyes and walked off the dock.

Chapter 6: Failure

The water hit me like a ton of bricks, because I wasn't expecting it. I sank for only a short while before my instincts kicked in and I swam to the surface. It didn't work. I was still there, only soaking wet.

I don't get it, I complained. *Maybe it didn't work because it wasn't a full moon?* I looked up at the sky. It was dark now, and the moon was nearly full, but not quite exactly full. Tomorrow. Tomorrow it would be a full moon. I'd have to come back and try again then.

I swam to shore lazily, and searched for my backpack on the grass. When I spotted it, thanks to the moon's light, I grabbed it and quickly unzipped it. I'd thrown a sweatshirt in there in case it got cold. Now that I was soaking wet, the dry sweatshirt would come in handy.

I quickly pulled off my soaking wet shirt and put on the dry sweatshirt. There. That felt better. I wrung out the wet shirt and stuffed it back inside my backpack. Then, I zipped it back up and headed back home.

Was I discouraged that the wormhole didn't work tonight? A little, yes. But I hadn't taken into account the moon. I should have waited to try tomorrow night. That was my next plan.

Chapter 7: Graduation Day

I woke up to my dad and Camden blowing party horns and bursting into my bedroom like they were walking in some sort of parade. They were wearing party hats and prancing around like crazy people.

"Rise and shine," my dad said cheerfully.

"Dad!" I moaned. I was exhausted. I looked over at my alarm clock. It was past 8 AM. I was usually up by now, but really enjoyed sleeping in on the weekends. I quickly grabbed a pillow and put it over my face to block out the noise.

"Today's your big day, Claire!" Camden shouted excitedly. He was just as enthused as my dad.

"What?" I asked. I sat up slowly and looked out the window. Was it my birthday? No, that was in August. It was still June the last time I remembered..

"Graduation day! I still can't believe it! My little girl is all grown up and graduating high school!" my dad sat on the edge of my bed.

Graduation day!?! I had literally completely forgotten all about graduation. *Crap*, I thought. *This is going to interfere with my time traveling plans.*

Was I excited to graduate? You bet! I couldn't wait to not have to report to school every day and have everyone stare at me. I was like a science project gone wrong that nobody could figure out. Plus, with my studies behind me, I could focus exclusively on Benjamin.

"Oh yeah.. Graduation day!" I tried to muster up as much excitement as I could. Truth was, I was excited. I just had a lot of planning to do and it was taking my mind off of the day's festivities.

"We've got a full day of events," Dad reminded me. "You've got the senior brunch at 11 AM, and then pictures in your cap and gown at 1 PM, and the graduation ceremony starts at 3 PM. Then, of course, is the Post-Graduation Party at the school, which starts with a banquet-type dinner at 5 PM." He was reading off of the itinerary the school must have sent.

Dad was right. There was so much to do today. I wouldn't have any time to think about my new plan. I started feeling hopeless again, but shook the feeling off as quickly as it set in. I owed this to my dad. I'd disappeared twice on him now, and I was his first kid to ever graduate highschool. I needed to go through the motions and let him be proud of me for once.

So, that's what I did. I got up, showered, and brushed my teeth. I even put a little bit of makeup on. I curled my hair and got dressed, and headed to the senior brunch. The brunch was held at a restaurant in town called *The Seagull*. It was owned by one of the senior's parents. I met Jacquelyn ahead of time and we walked in together.

Brunch was actually very delicious. I had pancakes with fresh strawberries, tomato soup and fresh baked bread, a beautiful tossed salad, and a big bowl of tropical fruit. I finished it off with a yogurt parfait - yum!

Jacquelyn seemed excited to be graduating, although she was nervous about her valedictorian speech. I told her she'd be awesome, and that she looked great, so not to worry. Easier said than done, I know.

After brunch, we headed to get our pictures taken in our caps and gowns. Most of the girls wore dresses, but I'd forgotten to shave my legs that morning, so I just threw on a pair of slacks. I smiled as widely as I could for the photographer when it was my turn. When he told me to throw my hat up in the air for one photo, I thought it was kind of corny, but I did it with as much enthusiasm as I could muster.

Before I knew it, it was nearly time for our graduation ceremony. I was excited, and also relieved. The quicker I could be done with this, the sooner I could finish out my plan and be with Benjamin once and for all.

"Are you sure you liked the part about us each finding our own path? You didn't think that was too cliche?" Jacquelyn talked even faster than normal when she was really nervous. She had been practicing her speech all day.

"I thought the whole thing was great!" I told her. Was it cliche? Absolutely. Speeches are always cliche. But it was perfectly appropriate and I knew all the seniors and their families would love it.

Jacquelyn sighed. She seemed relieved. We waited on stage for our names to be called in front of hundreds of people.

"And next, we have Trenton High's Class of 2021's Valedictorian, Jacquelyn Petrosino." Our principal announced enthusiastically.

Jacquelyn smiled at me and got up to head to the podium. As she spoke, I could see the pride in so many family's faces. I spotted my dad and Camden and knew that they were proud of me, too. What a milestone. Four years. And it all ends with one night like tonight. Life is strange.

As Jacquelyn finished her speech, people stood and clapped loudly. It was a huge hit! She had gotten a standing ovation! I was so happy for her.

Soon, it was time to get our diplomas. I was nearly last - as they were given out alphabetically. Finally, it was my turn.

"Claire Walker," our principal announced. I stood up and headed to shake his hand. I could see some of the seniors snicker to one another as I walked by. I noticed a few members of the audience whispering as well. I was the girl who'd disappeared twice with no good rhyme or reason. They all thought I was a huge weirdo, but I didn't care. I was doing this for my dad and brother.

I shook our principal's hand and grabbed my diploma. I held it up high as my dad snapped a picture of me on his phone. I heard Camden cheering loudly. Then, I headed back to my seat.

One more thing... I thought. It was the Post Graduation Party. It started with dinner at 5 PM for seniors and their families, and then there was a party in the gymnasium with vendors from all over. Last year, I'd heard they had a bounce house, cotton candy, and all sorts of carnival-themed stuff. I wondered what this year's party would look like.

At dinner, my dad must have told me a dozen times how proud he was of me. All three of us ate a pasta dish with a side salad and some garlic knots. For desert, we had cheesecake with fresh whipped cream and blackberry drizzle.

"And if your mom was here..." my dad began. I quickly swallowed the food in my mouth. I didn't like to talk about my mom. Of course, I loved her. But she died a really long time ago, and the thought made me so sad. She'd missed my graduation, and all of my life milestones. I let my dad continue, in case he had something he needed to get off his chest.

"She would just be so proud. She was always so proud of you, Claire," he continued. I smiled sweetly.

"This has been great, Dad. It's been really fun," I told him. I wanted him to think I was fully present, enjoying every moment of this special day.

"I'm glad," he said.

We continued eating, telling jokes from time to time, and just enjoying the moment. I realized that if I found a way to time travel, like I'd hoped, I'd be leaving my family again. This would be the third time I'd be away from Dad. I didn't know if he could take that. I quickly thought of a lie to cover my bases, just in case.

"So now that I'm officially a high school graduate, I was hoping to treat myself to a little trip," I started.

"Oh yeah, with who?" Dad inquired.

"I actually was hoping to go alone. It's kind of a therapeutic trip. There's a college I wanted to visit. I was going to bring my journal and just spend some time in nature, maybe do a yoga class. Stuff like that" I lied.

"What college?" he asked.

There was a community college not too far. It was about an hour away, which gave me an excuse to be gone but wouldn't give my dad a heart attack.

"Whitesburg County Community College," I lied again. "They have a pretty solid journalism program I was hoping to ask about."

"Hmm.." my dad seemed surprised. "I thought you'd go for math - that was always your best subject."

"I might," I said. "They have a math major, too. I just need to do some research, that's all," I said. I felt bad lying. In fact, I felt bad that I even had to lie. Everybody else knew what their college plans were in April. But I was gone and kidnapped on a pirate ship trapped in a time loop, so I hadn't really had time to think about it.

"When were you planning on leaving?" Dad asked.

"I was actually hoping to head out later this evening," I had to make the lie believable in case later this evening, I was nowhere to be found - in this century, at least.

"Well," Dad said, "You're a highschool graduate now. It's good that you're looking at some colleges. Stay safe and call us when you get there."

I smiled. Then I looked at Camden. He was pushing his food around on his plate with his fork. His eyes told me he knew I was lying. I couldn't bear to look at them.

"Great!" I said. "I'm actually going to see if I can find Jacquelyn. Maybe she'd want to come?" I said, standing up and pushing in my chair. Really, I just wanted to get fresh air and get away from Camden's accusing stares.

Dad nodded.

I quickly headed outside and searched up in the sky. I saw the moon, full as could be. It was breathtaking. It was also a little scary, knowing the power that he had.

It was starting to get darker. I searched the water for signs of a ship. I was shocked when I found one, just anchored at the end of the pier. It wasn't the Serpent's Skull, and it wasn't the Golden Green. How many mystical pirate ships were there?

I knew I should stay away, but I couldn't. My heart pulled me towards it. *Claire*, my brain yelled, *you've done this twice before and both times you almost died. Stop!* But you know me, my brain rarely wins out over my heart these days.

I slowly headed towards the ship. It was much smaller than the other ships I'd been on. But the men were definitely stuck in the same time loop as Benjamin.

Benjamin… my sweet, sweet love. What if I could get on this ship and find him, somewhere out there in the deep blue sea of the 1800s?

But wouldn't that mess up my time travel plans with the wormhole? I stared up at the moon. I didn't know for sure that the wormhole idea would work. It certainly didn't work yesterday. My brain started calculating. If the wormhole idea didn't work, I'd have to wait a whole month for another full moon to try any other plan. I had no patience. I didn't want to wait.

Suddenly, it was as if my plans were thrown out the window. I didn't even care about time travelling. I only cared about being with Benjamin, at that very moment. And for every moment for all of eternity.

I stood behind some brush, hiding as low to the ground as I could. I watched as men unloaded some cargo from the ship. I saw them toss what looked like a body off to the side of the pier. It landed on the sand below. I peered over and saw a man. He was still alive, but heavily intoxicated. His clothes were tattered and dirty, and he reeked something fierce.

Don't ask me what I was thinking, but I suddenly had an idea. I knew how I could get on that ship. I took off my shirt and wiped the makeup off my face. Then, I climbed down and took the man's shirt and hat. I twirled my hair up into a bun. I quickly climbed into the dirty, old clothes and placed his hat on my head. And then I took a deep breath and walked onto a strange pirate ship, for the third time.

Chapter 8: Just Playing The Part

I know, I know, I'm a crazy person. I see a therapist and everything. I don't know why I am the way I am, except.. I am madly, hopelessly in love with a man and would do anything - and I mean anything - to be with him.

So there I was, on a pirate ship, pretending to be a pirate. Luckily for me, I'd been around pirates long enough to know their mannerisms, and the language they used. I knew about the jobs they completed, too. This wouldn't be too hard for me. I would just have to keep playing the part.

"Hey lad!" One of them called to me.

"Ay?" I answered. I had already grabbed a few jugs from the dock and brought them on board with me. I needed to look busy and not suspicious.

"Put those over here!" he shouted. I nodded and followed his direction. I continued helping others stack crates and jugs of supplies.

"You new, lad?" someone asked.

"Ay, just boarded," I said. "Ready for some treasure hunting!" I added, trying to sound like a pirate as best as I could. I knew that some pirates would get off the ships when they docked, and others would get on. I hoped they wouldn't find me suspicious.

The pirate chuckled. He seemed friendly. "There ain't no treasure on this ship," he said, laughing.

I smirked and continued to carry the cargo up the ramp and down into what I assume was the storage room. Nobody else really paid much attention to me.

A few hours later, the same pirate from earlier came to sit next to me as I rested on the deck.

"What's your name, lad?" he asked, taking a swig of his flask. It was obviously rum.

"James," I replied. It was the first name I could think of, and a name I knew was popular in the 1800s.

"Well, it's nice to have ye with us, James," he said, sticking his hand out to shake mine.

I realized I still had nailpolish on, and thought it best not to shake his hand. I also wasn't very strong and assumed I had a girly hand-shake. He might find me suspicious then.

The man's name was Thomas, or at least that's what he told me to call him. I'd learned that it was common for pirates (and criminals, in general) to use an alias. He was kind to me, treating me almost like a son.

* **

Laboring aboard a pirate ship was hard work. The sun was hot and the days were long. I couldn't stand the way I reeked day after day. But I had my eye on the prize: Benjamin. I was determined to find him.

The days were busy and full of tough, manual labor. I almost felt bad for the crew having all this work to do while the Captain mostly drank rum and steered the ship from time to time - *almost*. But they knew what they were signing up for - free food and shelter, and a chance to find (ahem, *steal*) some valuable stuff. Eventually, I heard of plans to dock the ship. I knew this would be the perfect opportunity to put my plan into full speed ahead. If I could get off the ship and find a gypsy, someone other than Genevieve, I could inquire about another way to break the curse.

I believed Genevieve was being honest with Benjamin when she told him that she didn't see another way; that he'd have to end my life. But that was only what *she* saw, and maybe her powers were limited. Maybe there was a more powerful gypsy out there. Surely, there *had* to be another way.

Chapter 9: On The Hunt

As soon as the boat docked, I waited by the other crew members anxiously wanting to get off. But, I didn't want to seem too eager or suspicious.

"You gettin' off?" Thomas asked.

"Ay, for a bit," I said in response.

We followed the crowd down and off the ship. It felt good to set my feet on the dock. I couldn't wait to walk on actual land. I didn't understand how pirates could stand being on a boat for weeks at a time. Some of them spent their entire lives on one!

There were many small tents set up along the shore. I looked around for some sign of gypsies. I knew they were popular during this time. But I also knew that for many, they were frowned upon. I remembered Captain Brooks telling me "witches are evil". So, I assumed they wouldn't necessarily be advertising their services out in the open.

I walked in and out of quite a few tents. Many merchants were selling bottles of what I assumed were alcohol. There were also merchants selling clothing, jewels, and food.

Finally, I walked into a tent where there was a young-ish woman selling bread and a middle-aged woman standing in the corner, watching the customers carefully. I noticed her necklace and immediately knew what she was: a gypsy. She wore a necklace similar to Genevieve's. It was made of the bones of many small animals.

The woman looked me over curiously. I still resembled a boy.

"Hello," I said, walking up to her. I was certain she would see through my costume. Gypsies just had a way of *knowing* things.

"Hello there," she responded, not moving.

"I was wondering if you could help me with something," I said, softly. I glanced around. There were no other customers inside the tent with us, just a few passing by on the outside.

"You want help with the impossible," she stated. She started playing with a bracelet on her wrist; rolling the beads back and forth across her hand.

I wasn't surprised in the least that she seemed to know what I wanted help with before I even asked. Genevieve had always been able to know what I wanted before I asked.

"Please," I begged, whispering now. "It's really important to me."

She looked me over before smirking.

"You will not like the outcome," she simply said.

"I have to try!" I practically shouted, though in a whisper.

"Very well then," she motioned for me to follow her behind a curtain. I looked around to see if anyone was watching, and then I walked into a small room with a round table and two chairs. It looked eerily similar to the palm reader's room in Trenton.

"Does that costume fool them?" she said, mockingly.

"Yes, actually. So far it has," I said. I didn't know how much longer I could keep up the charade, but I was hoping this woman could help me and that it would all be over soon.

"Men are so naive," she simply stated. "Come, sit." She beckoned me to sit in one of the chairs as she took a seat in the chair across it. She crossed her legs and then her arms.

"Tell me what bothers you," she said calmly, though I was certain she likely knew much of it.

I took off my hat and let my long, pale hair fall around my face. The gypsy didn't flinch.

"I'm in love with a man - a pirate. His name is Benjamin. But he's cursed. My ancestor actually put the curse on him. To break the curse, he'd have to end my life. So we can never be together. But, there has to be another way. Maybe I could time travel and stop the curse from happening in the first place," I said, listening to the words as they left my mouth. I sounded crazed but I didn't care.

"You inquire about time travel?" she asked. She continued to play with the beads on her bracelet.

"Yes," I said. "I'd like to go back to the time and place moments before the curse happened. If I could stop it from happening, Benjamin would be free."

"Timelines are very fragile. One small change changes everything. You would change *everything*," she said, not blinking. I remembered the palm reader telling me the same thing.

I didn't care. I had to break the curse. I had to be with Benjamin.

"I don't care," I told her. "Please, I'm desperate. Can you help me?" I pleaded.

She looked me over again. I could tell she was undecided. I simply stared her in the eyes and prayed that she could feel the determination inside me.

"Very well," she said. I couldn't believe my ears! Was she actually going to help me?!

"I can show you where a wormhole is. If I take you there, you will need to know exactly which moment you plan to return to."

I nodded, listening intensely.

"It will cost you a fair price, of course," she added. *Crap*, I thought.

I hadn't thought of how I would pay her. I reached into my pants pockets to pull out whatever I could find. There was only my graduation program, folded, crinkled, and practically falling apart. I showed her. She laughed.

"You ask to travel back in time and that is what you offer me?" she sounded disgusted.

"I'm so sorry.." I started, "I've just been so focused on doing this so that I could be with the man I love, it completely slipped my mind to figure out a way that I could compensate you." It was the truth.

She looked at me disgustedly, but then her eyes fell to my necklace - the small, gold cross that Camden had gifted me a while back. I never took it off. It gave me hope when he went missing.

"How about your necklace?" she asked, nodding to it.

"I'm sorry," I quickly replied, holding it tightly in my fisted grip. Although I loved Benjamin and would do practically anything for him, I also loved my little brother earnestly. "My little brother gave this to me; it's special. I love him too much to give it away."

"Love is a crazy thing," she said, looking off into the distance.

"It sure is," I said, my head still hanging. I was devastated. I finally found someone who could help me, and I had no way to pay her.

Suddenly, the gypsy surprised me.

"I'll tell you what," she said. "I will take you to the wormhole. But I warn you: anything you touch, or anyone you talk to, you will forever change the future."

I could tell she felt bad for me. I secretly wondered if she also loved someone and recognized the determination inside of me.

"I understand," I said, reaching out my hand to shake hers. She looked at my hand and smiled, never extending her own.

"Let us leave now," she said, quickly standing. She wrapped a scarf around her hair and headed towards the opening in the tent.

Chapter 10: Mazes And Magic Mirrors

I stood up to follow her. I quickly wrapped my hair in a tight bun and shoved my hat back on. Then, I ran out of the tent to find her. She moved quickly, weaving in and out of people walking in the opposite direction. It was hard to keep up with her.

Eventually, she turned to head down a slim, dark alley. It was situated between two stone buildings. The smell of alcohol almost knocked me out as I entered it. I could only assume the buildings were taverns. There was nobody else in the alleyway except for the gypsy and me.

I was practically running to keep up with her. A few times, I had to jump over a pile of things or swerve to avoid running into something.

"Miss!" I called out, hoping she would slow down. If I lost sight of her, I would be completely lost. Not only would I not know how to get to the wormhole, but I wouldn't even be able to make it back to the ship!

She did not even turn to me when I called her. She simply kept walking, even faster than she was before. Eventually, she pushed through a wooden door at the end of the alley and walked inside. I feared that I would lose her. I literally ran as fast as I could until I got to the same door, pushing it open.

Inside there was a small room, no bigger than a large closet. There was a tall mirror leaning against the wall in the corner. The room was dark. I saw the mirror and the gypsy only when she lit a candle.

"There," she said, pointing to the mirror. It was taller than me, with beautiful gold edging. The gypsy stared at the candle's flame.

"Wha, what do I do?" I asked, nervously.

She smiled. "Where do you want to go?" she inquired.

"I want to go back in time to the place where my ancestor was putting a curse on Benjamin's ship," I told her.

She giggled slightly. "Don't tell me, tell the mirror," she said. "And then go." She nodded towards the mirror.

I turned to face the mirror. It was exquisite; absolutely breathtaking. I was not surprised that it was special enough to possess a magical quality such as time travel.

I cleared my throat. How silly I would look, talking to a mirror. But I would do anything for Benjamin.

"I want to go back in time. I want to go to the place where Arabelle placed a curse on Captain Stanton's ship. I want to arrive minutes before she places the curse," I told the mirror. I was surprised at how confident I sounded. I was not usually a confident person. Reckless? Determined? Absolutely.

"Now you go," the gypsy whispered. I could see her reflection in the giant mirror. Was I supposed to walk through the mirror? It sounded absurd, but it also felt right. I reached out my pointer finger to touch the mirror. Surprisingly, it penetrated the glass. Frightened, I quickly pulled it back.

I took a deep breath. This was scary. It was unknown territory. I mustered up all the courage I could, and then I took one giant step forward, into the mirror. *For Benjamin*, I told myself.

Chapter 11: Stop!

My eyes were closed as I continued to walk into the past. It was the strangest feeling. It felt like everything was floating, like there was no gravity. I felt like my arms and legs didn't really belong to me; like they weren't attached. It didn't feel like walking through air; it felt like something else. Something that I couldn't describe. Some type of half liquid/half gas substance that hadn't been discovered yet.

I continued to walk and eventually opened my eyes when I heard birds chipping.

I had made it. I was there, on the pier. I saw The Serpent's Skull. I breathed in the salty air of the ocean. I remembered this place from when Genevieve sent me back in time. This was definitely it.

I looked around quickly. I didn't know how much time I had. I had only asked for a few minutes before the curse was placed; maybe I should have asked for more time. I ran to the place where I remembered Arabelle hiding. I had to find her, and quickly.

My long hair flowed along my back as I ran as quickly as I could. I saw Captain Stantun step off of his ship and onto the dock and I knew I didn't have much time. Arabelle's friends and family were already lined up, with pirates holding them hostage with swords.

I hid behind whatever I could find, trying to make my way to her. Eventually, I got there. Surprisingly, I wasn't afraid. Even though I knew she was a witch. Even though I knew that she was capable of putting horrible curses on people, I was not afraid in the slightest. It was odd.

"Arabelle?" I breathed. I had found her before Stanton did, thank goodness.

She looked up at me, with a gentleness in her eyes. Then she spoke.

"What are you doing here, child?" she asked. Her voice was so kind; she sounded like an angel.

"I came to stop you," I whispered. "If you put a curse on Captain Stanton's ship, you'll put a curse on his son - Benjamin. And I love him."

She smiled. "You are foolish, girl. Love makes you do crazy things," she said.

I heard Stanton's boots getting closer.

"You don't understand," I tried to tell her, rushing. "The only way for Benjamin to break the curse would be to end my life, and he won't do that. We end up falling in love. But we can never be together," I added. I hadn't really thought this plan through, I realized, as I hurriedly tried to convince her not to curse Stanton. I was just hoping to talk to her and that maybe she would understand.

"This is not your time, child," Arabelle said, reaching out her hand to touch my cheek. I felt a sense of peace as she cradled my cheek. I knew she knew we were related. Her hands were stained with blood from the injury she'd recently suffered. "You must go back."

"I cannot!" I stated. "I won't. Not until I know that Benjamin will be free."

"Oh child, if you change the past, you change the future. The whole future," she said, sounding centuries smarter and wiser than me. How many times were these gypsies going to tell me that?

"I'm willing to take that chance," I told her. "But please, do not curse Stanton." Speaking of Stanton, his boots were loudly stomping on the deck and I knew that he was right around the corner. If I didn't hurry and get out of there, he'd likely kill me too. Then I'd have no future to return to. I had no time left.

What a shame. There I was, sharing a moment in time with my great-great grandmother. How I wish we had more time. I would have loved to ask her so many questions. But we had no time. She had no time. And I had to get out of there.

I kissed her forehead and squeezed her hand before standing up to leave.

I quickly ran to hide on the other side of some large supply bags. I prayed that Stanton wouldn't find me.

It was horrible, having to listen to my ancestor go through the same death experience for the second time. But she didn't hum this time. And Stanton didn't cough, as he did before when she blew the powder into his face. I could only hope that this meant Arabelle decided against placing the curse on him.

I waited for the sound of steel toed boots to wander off into the distance. As soon as he was gone, I got up and ran to find my way back to the magical mirror.

I ran to where I was when I first opened my eyes on the pier. But there was no mirror. I started to panic. It looked around. I saw a long alleyway between two buildings about thirty yards away. I quickly ran to it. I noticed people looking at me oddly as I made my way through. Eventually, I got to the end of the alley and found a door. I pushed it open.

Chapter 12: Old Friends

But there was no mirror. Just a small, dark room. I panicked. I felt myself start to hyperventilate. I had no idea how I was going to return to my own time. I started running my hands over the stone walls, hoping my fingers would penetrate part of it. But it was no use.

"Looking for this?" an old haggard woman said screechily from the corner of the room. She held up a small mirror. Her voice startled me, but also brought with it a sense of comfort.

"Genevieve?" I asked. She smiled, showing her many missing teeth. Apparently, Genevieve hadn't been kidnapped by Stanton and his crew yet. I wondered if he'd kidnapped her after finding out that he was cursed. He probably kidnapped many gypsies in an attempt to break the curse. But now, would Genevieve ever make it aboard The Serpent's Skull? The thought made me a little sad. I knew that Benjamin adored her, and considered her almost like a mother-type figure.

"What took you so long?" she chuckled. I laughed.

"I couldn't figure it out," I told her. "Once I knew I'd have to time travel, I tried asking for help from a palm reader but it didn't work out..." I started to explain what had happened. But, there was no point. I could tell from Genevieve's expression that she already knew what I'd been through.

"I've been waiting and waiting," she said, still holding the mirror. It had the same beautiful golden edging as the tall mirror I'd walked through.

"I'm sorry," I told her.

"Don't be sorry," she said. "You set us all free, Claire. Stanton, Benjamin, me…"

I hadn't realized that my preventing the curse on The Serpent's Skull would keep Genevieve from being imprisoned. That was a bonus, and I was glad to be able to help her.

I smiled, but Genevieve's expression turned sad.

"Of course, when you alter the past, you also change the future," she said, in a sad voice.

"Yes, I know," I said. I'd been told that how many times?!

She smiled. "Very well, then." She held up the mirror to face me. "Where do you want to go?" she asked.

I thought for a moment. I wanted to be with Benjamin, that was undeniable. But I also felt sadness, leaving my dad and Camden without even saying goodbye. I couldn't do that, not again. Not for the third and final time. I had to get back to Trenton. I could say my goodbyes, and I would tell them I was leaving for college. Then, I would go to be with Benjamin.

"I want to go to present day Trenton, to see my father and my brother."

Genevieve smiled, but her eyes were hiding something that I couldn't quite put my finger on.

"Go, then," she said, still holding the mirror. I wondered how I was supposed to walk through that tiny mirror. I reached my left hand out and felt the familiar sense of my fingers penetrating the glass. I closed my eyes and took a big, confident step forward.

When I opened my eyes, I was on the beach in Trenton.

Chapter 13: Back To The Present

I breathed in the familiar salty air. I felt the familiar breeze on my skin. I smiled. I was home. I reached down to grab a handful of sand and felt it slide out of my fingertips. There was a sense of calm surrounding me, and I felt blissful.

I hurried home to find my Dad and Camden. They were in the kitchen, baking cookies.

"Claire!" Camden yelled excitedly as I walked through the door. I gave him a huge hug as he ran to me.

"Hey, bud!" I said. Then I got low enough and whispered, "Sorry I had to go away again."

Camden looked confused.

"Hey, Claire," my dad said enthusiastically. "We just finished baking some chocolate chip cookies. They need to cool for a few minutes. Would you like one?"

That's odd, I thought. *I'd been gone for weeks. Didn't they miss me?*

"Don't you want to know where I was?" I asked, confused.

My dad looked confused. "Weren't you at Jacquelyn's?" he asked.

For weeks? When did I ever go to Jacquelyn's for weeks, and without calling home?

"Yeah," I simply said, looking at Camden. But he didn't seem concerned that I had been gone either. *What is going on?* I thought.

"Yeah, I'll take a cookie," I said, "I just need to grab something from my room. I'll be right back." I grabbed a cookie, shoved it in my mouth and quickly headed to my bedroom.

I picked up the phone and dialed Jacquelyn's number.

"Hey, girl!" my best friend squealed. "What's up?"

"Hey!" I said. "Did you cover for me or something?" I asked, wondering if she'd told my dad I was at her house so he wouldn't ask too many questions.

"What are you talking about?" she asked, in a confused voice.

"This last time, when I went missing.. My dad thought I was at your house," I tried to explain. Suddenly, there was a horrible feeling in my gut.

"You were at my house, Claire. You spent the night last night," she said. "What's going on?"

The feeling in my gut grew stronger.

"But before that, where was I?" I asked, panicked now.

"I don't know.. Probably at your house?" she said, more confused than ever.

"Jacquelyn.. Where did we disappear to earlier this year? We were gone for months, and our families were worried sick. Where were we?" I whispered.

"Claire," the voice on the other end said, "Are you okay?"

"Just answer the question," I demanded. I literally felt the vomit rising.

"Claire, I have no idea what you're talking about. When did we ever *disappear*?"

I took a deep breath and closed my eyes. Was it possible that in this new timeline, Jacquelyn and I were never kidnapped by pirates?

"You know what, I'm not feeling that great. I think it was something I ate. I'm sorry, Jacquelyn. I'll call you back later," I said, hanging up the phone.

"Hey Cam," I shouted to my younger brother. "Can you come here for a second?"

Camden was the first of us to be kidnapped, at least in the timeline I originated from.

Camden came into my room, eating a chocolate chip cookie and with a huge smile.

"Hey, so.. My therapist wanted me to just go over some things with you," I started.

"Your what?" he said.

"My therapist," I repeated.

"What's a therapist?" he asked. But that was impossible - he knew very well what a therapist was. Our whole family was in therapy after the ordeals we'd been through!

I shook my head quickly. I'd try another route.

"Do you ever have nightmares about being kidnapped?" I asked him.

"No, I don't think so," Camden replied innocently. "I have nightmares about zombies, though!" He giggled.

"I mean, about the pirates," I suggested.

He looked at me like I had ten heads.

"What pirates?" he asked. This time I had to swallow the vomit back down. Was Camden never kidnapped by pirates? Were none of us ever kidnapped?

"Last year, when you went missing…" I tried to spark his memory.

"Missing?" he repeated. And that's when I knew. I knew what I'd done.

I'd prevented Benjamin from being cursed, which was my goal from the beginning. Unfortunately, I didn't realize that if his ship was never cursed, they wouldn't be stuck in a time loop. They would live their lives out just like the rest of us. There would be no full moon bringing them to the dock to kidnap people in a different time. Benjamin would have been able to get off The Serpent's Skull whenever he wanted to, and he most likely did. I would have never met him. He would have lived his life centuries before I was even born. There would be no Benjamin in my life.

Chapter 14: I Cannot Be Stopped

I laid on my back in my bed, in shock. I was devastated. Had I really just gone through everything I'd gone through for nothing? I would never get to see or be with Benjamin - not ever! I laid there for what seemed like an eternity, just empty and broken.

They were right - all of the gypsies and the palm reader. When you change one small thing in the past, it changes so many things in the future. I wish I would have listened.

But then again, part of me was glad. I did love Benjamin, even if we'd never even met in this timeline. The thought of him being cursed broke my heart into a million pieces. At least I was able to free him from that. He must have lived a normal life. I hoped he was happy. I wondered if he ever settled down with anyone...

My father and Camden became worried about me. They wanted to know why all of a sudden, I wouldn't leave my room. I wasn't eating. I was thoroughly depressed.

Jacquelyn offered to take me on a shopping spree. My dad said he'd take me to look at a few different colleges. Camden wanted to go fishing and to play outside. But nothing would make me feel better, as hard as they might try. There was only one thing I wanted; one thing I absolutely *needed*: Benjamin.

A week went by and I was still reeling the loss of my one true love. *How pathetic*, I thought, *that I'm pining over a man who doesn't even know that I exist.* But it didn't change the way I felt about him. I knew that was real. It didn't matter which timeline it was or whether our paths crossed or not. My love for Benjamin was real.

Eventually, as I always do when I'm bound and determined, I came up with a plan. If I'd gone into the past to stop the curse from being placed, why couldn't I go into the past to see Benjamin? I could try, at least. It was the perfect time in my present day life: I was getting ready to go off to college. My family wouldn't even realize I was gone.

I thought about the idea for a few days, and when I no longer felt the will to live without him, I decided to at least *try*.

I remembered where the palm reader had said she believed there was a wormhole. It was on the end of the dock about a half mile away. The problem was, I tried it before and it didn't work. But, it wasn't a full moon that night. She had specifically remembered a customer using it during the full moon. I decided it didn't hurt to try again. I looked at my calendar and noticed that the next full moon was a week away.

That gave me plenty of time to spend good, quality time with the people in this timeline that I loved. I'd go fishing with Camden and take hikes with my dad and go shopping with Jacquelyn. After all, if everything worked out, I hoped to be with Benjamin forever. I figured, since his time was centuries before mine, I could spend a lifetime with him and then still come back to my own time. I didn't know if that was how it worked, but that was my plan at least.

It was magical, that last week with my loved ones. How much more you cherish each second when you know you won't see someone for a very long time. I wish more people could experience that during their daily interactions. For me, I thoroughly enjoyed each moment and made sure to lock them away in my heart and memory forever.

On the night of the full moon, I headed towards the wormhole. This time, I didn't bring a backpack with me. I knew this was it; my last chance. My last plan. If this didn't work, then I didn't know what I was going to do.

I looked up at the sky. It was crystal clear; navy blue with a huge, glowing moon. It was breathtaking. I smiled. I longed to gaze up at it with Benjamin's arms wrapped tightly around me.

I looked at the end of the dock. There was no magic mirror. There was nothing; just water below. I took a deep breath and started walking towards the nothingness. When I reached the end of the dock, I closed my eyes.

"I want to go to the time of Benjamin Stanton, Captain of The Serpent's Skull." I took a step and felt that familiar eerie half liquid/half gas substance surrounding me. It was my cue to keep walking. I kept my eyes closed, and continued walking. Suddenly, I felt a bright light on my eyelids. I slowly opened them.

Chapter 15: Long Lost Love

The sun was shining and birds were chirping. I looked around quickly, but knew from experience that I was standing on the deck of a pirate ship. Ahead of me was a tall, handsome man with sandy brown hair and a Captain's hat.

"Benjamin", I breathed. I couldn't believe my eyes. The wormhole had actually worked! He turned his head slightly, and looked at me cautiously.

His expression turned utterly confused.

"How do you know my name, Miss?" He asked. My heart broke. I literally felt it tear right in half at that very moment. Of course, after I understood that I messed with the past in a way that would change the future, I realized Benjamin and I would have never met in this timeline. As happy as I was that he was no longer cursed and that he was able to leave his ship without experiencing excruciating pain, I was the one experiencing excruciating pain. It was like we'd been *erased* - our relationship and our love. The palm reader in Trenton was right - I made things even more miserable, for me, at least.

How could I answer his question? Could I tell him everything that had happened? Would he believe me? He'd never even been cursed in this timeline, so would he believe in things like witches, and palm readers, and magic? I felt hopeless, and this time, there was no way to shake the feeling.

I stayed silent, but walked towards him. I could feel the tears streaming down my cheeks. I hoped that even though his brain wouldn't recognize me, maybe his heart would feel *something*.

Anything.

He simply watched me walk. He looked curious. Soon, I was standing right in front of him.

"Are you hurt, Miss?" he asked, watching the tears fall down my face freely. He looked concerned.

I simply shook my head no.

"Have we met before?" He asked, curiously. *Oh, Benjamin*, I thought. How I longed to tell him everything. I wanted to tell him all about the first time we met, and how he'd made me leave him twice because he loved me, but that I was determined to be with him and was willing to do anything and everything to make that happen.

I wanted to hold him, to grab him and to never let go. But to him, I was a stranger.

"A long time ago," I answered him. It was the truth. We had fallen in love less than a year ago, but in a different timeline. One that no longer existed. One that was *erased.*

"I don't recall," he said honestly. He waited for me to explain. But I didn't know what to say. I just stared at him, hoping to spark some memory inside of him.

"Are you from the shore? Do you need safe passage?" He asked. He was still such a sweet soul.

"I am from the shore," I told him. "And no, I'm not travelling. I just came to see you," I told him honestly.

His eyes squinted and he looked even more confused than before.

"Are you hungry?" he asked, after a few moments of silence.

I was starving. He must have heard my stomach rumbling.

"Yes, actually," I said, honestly. "I'm starving!"

"Let me get you some nourishment," he said, kindly. He turned and headed down towards the galley.

I walked over to the railing on the ship, looking out onto the shore. It broke my heart that Benjamin had no recollection of me, but I wondered if we could fall in love again.

A few minutes later, he brought up a plate full of fresh fruit. I looked at it, confused. Where was all the grey mush? I happily took the plate and started shoving the fruit in my mouth. It was delicious; perfectly ripe and sweeter than any fruit I'd ever tasted. I smiled as I ate it. I guess with no curse, Benjamin and his mates were able to get off the ship any time and get as much fresh food as they could possibly want. At least that was a positive. No more grey mush holding them over from one full moon to the next.

"You *were* hungry," he observed. "When was the last time you ate something?" he asked.

I couldn't remember. I shrugged.

He pulled a flask from his coat pocket. "Here, have a drink," he said, handing it to me. I grabbed it and drank. It was water. Benjamin never was a big drinker.

"Would you like more?" he asked, staring at the plate I'd just emptied in less than a minute.

"No thanks," I said, slightly embarrassed.

"What did you say your name was?" he asked.

"Claire," I replied. "Claire Walker." I suddenly felt a flashback to the first time he'd asked me for my name.

"It's nice to meet you, Claire," he said, tipping his hat down just a tad. "Or, to meet you again," he added.

"It's always been my pleasure," I assured him. He made a strange face but then smiled.

"Is there something I can help you with?" he asked. I assumed he was confused as to what I was doing there. I'd already told him I wasn't planning on travelling.

"I, uh," cue the nervous stuttering, "I came to see you," I told him. It was so hard not to run to him and tell him everything all at once. I knew he was a kind man, no matter which timeline he was on. But, would he believe anything I had to say?

"How can I help you?" he asked again, clearly very confused. Just then, a very pretty girl headed over to us.

"Hello," she said sweetly. My heart stopped. Was this Benjamin's girlfriend? I hadn't even thought about the possibility of him having met and fallen in love with someone else. I started to feel the fruit I'd just eaten creep back up into my throat and I had to swallow it back down.

"Hello," I replied back, as kindly as I could.

She looked at Benjamin and placed her hand on his shoulder. I immediately felt a rush of jealousy so heavy, it almost knocked me over.

"Do you need anything else, Captain?" she asked him.

He grabbed her hand, removing it from his overcoat, and placing it at her side.

"I think we're all set, Maria," he said in an even tone.

I walked over to the railing again and held on tight. I felt like I would pass out. Benjamin followed me.

"Miss Claire," he said, placing his hand gently on the small of my back. "Are you alright?"

"No," I told him truthfully. I looked back at Maria. She was stunning. Were the two of them in love? What right did anybody else have to Benjamin? Especially after everything I'd been through for the two of us to be together. I'd jumped timelines, for Pete's sake! I felt sick.

Genevieve was right about one thing. She always told Benjamin, "Thou shall lose thy love by thy own hand." It was true. Only Benjamin didn't realize he lost his love. But I did. And it was because of what I did - what I did with my own hand. And afterwards, the curse was broken. It was all so true. So true and so wicked.

"Please, come sit down," he beckoned me to go with him. I would have followed him anywhere. I slowly started to walk with him, but Maria followed us. If I was going to tell him anything, I couldn't have her there. Should I tell him everything that happened? What if he was happy with Maria?

"Actually, do you mind if we sit on the deck?" I asked.

He paused for a moment. "Of course," he said.

"And maybe we could speak privately?" I asked, afraid to hear his response. If he loved Maria the way he'd loved me, he'd be highly protective of her.

"Absolutely. Maria, could you give Claire and I a moment alone?" he asked her.

She smiled sweetly and nodded before heading back downstairs.

"Is that your girlfriend?" I asked, as soon as she was out of earshot. He was clearly taken back by my forwardness.

"What is a girlfriend?" he responded. I smiled. I missed how much I used to have to explain to him.

"You know.. A girl that you're in love with?" I explained. I bit my lip and waited. I hoped he'd say that they were just friends.

He blushed a little bit and put his head down. "I've known Maria since we were children. But no, I'm not in love with her," he answered. He looked back to the staircase where she'd gone below deck. "Why do you ask?"

"Because you used to be in love with me!" I shouted, speaking so fast my words slurred together. I couldn't help it. It just slipped out. I looked down at the water and shook my head.

Chapter 16: Pardon?

"**P**ardon?" was all he could say. He watched me, curiously.

I guess I'll just go for it, I thought. After all, what other choice did I have? I couldn't make him fall in love with me all over again with a beautiful girl like Maria always following him around. And I saw the way she touched his shoulder, she was definitely flirting with him.

"This is going to sound absolutely crazy," I told him, "but I assure you, it's the truth. You and I met less than a year ago. Your ship was under some crazy curse, because your father wasn't a nice man, and you were stuck in a time loop. I'm not from this time, I'm from the future," I paused and checked his expression. He was motionless. "Anyways, I was captured by your crew, and we fell in love. But you couldn't ever leave your ship. You were miserable. You wanted to leave so badly. And you didn't want me to be stuck on here with you. So you brought me back to shore so that I could live a happy, normal life. But I wasn't happy! I was miserable without you! I had to be with you, no matter what." I paused again.

Benjamin didn't move. He was frozen, like a statue. His eyes watched mine.

"So I found a way back to you, and we were happy and in love, but you refused to let me waste my life away on this ship, so you brought me back to the shore again. It would have been perfect if you could come with me, but because of the curse, you couldn't leave the ship. We were separated again, and I hated every second of it. So I devised a plan to break the curse. Well, actually, you could have broken the curse by ending my life. But you wouldn't do it. So I had to find a different way."

Benjamin looked beyond confused. He stood there, silent. I knew how I sounded: absolutely crazy.

"I realized if I could travel back in time to moments before the curse was placed, I could stop it. And then you'd be free." I looked down. "But I didn't realize that without the curse, I wouldn't have been kidnapped by your crew in the first place, and we'd never meet."

I started sobbing. Benjamin placed his hand on my shoulder, delicately.

"Please don't cry, Claire," he said softly. "It sounds like you've been through a lot. You must be tired. Would you like a place to rest?"

"I'm not tired! It's the truth!" I yelled. "You don't remember me because I altered the past. I had to, though. I couldn't stand the thought of you being cursed on this ship forever."

Benjamin took a deep breath.

"Is there nothing you feel when you look at me?" I was pleading now, pleading for him to remember *something*.

He paused for a moment before answering.

"I feel like I'm looking at someone who's determined.. And a bit reckless," he said. "You walked all the way onto this ship without knowing whether you'd be harmed," he explained. "There must be something that you're determined to have."

"Benjamin," I tried to explain, "I would do *anything* for you. Anything at all."

He looked down, a bit sheepishly.

"Ask me something!" I begged him. "We used to lay in your bed and we'd take turns telling each other everything about our lives." I tried to remind him.

"Alright then," he figured he'd play along. "What do you know about my father?" I had mentioned that his father was not a nice man.

"Captain Stanton," I began, "he was the most feared pirate in the sea. He was not kind, and he took many women as slaves."

"Well, he certainly has quite the reputation," Benjamin agreed. *Ugh, he thought I was just reciting what I'd heard about his reputation.*

"Ask me something else!" I encouraged. There had to be something about him that I knew that could prove I was telling the truth.

He thought for a moment. It was just long enough to give me an idea.

"You hate being a pirate!" I very nearly shouted at him. "You absolutely hate it! You hated the way your father acted and you long to live on the shore."

He squinted at me. There was no way for me to know that, unless he'd told it to me.

I continued to sob, praying that what I had said would spark some sort of memory in him.

He grabbed my hand on the railing and turned me to face him. He moved slowly, delicately. I held onto his hand tightly, and looked down as we held hands, smiling.

He looked me over curiously. Then he reached down to grab my hair. He ran his fingers through parts of it, never taking his eyes off mine.

"You mean to tell me," he said slowly, "that you loved me so much, you traveled through time to break a curse that kept us from being together."

"Yes!" I grabbed his face with both my hands. He reached up to hold his own hands over mine. He rubbed my fingers and looked at me concerningly.

"And now you don't even remember me," I sobbed. I moved my hands away from his face and onto the collar of his overcoat.

"Please don't get upset," he tried to comfort me. But it was no use. I was devastated.

"We were so in love, Benjamin. I mean, *passionately* in love," I told him. "I was only trying to make it so that we could be happy together forever. And now, I've messed it up." I sobbed some more.

Benjamin reached down to cradle my face.

"You didn't mess up anything, Claire," he tried to assure me.

"We'll never get that back," I told him. "It's gone. All of our memories are gone. Erased. Forever."

He stared deeply into my eyes.

"May I kiss you?" he asked, and by doing so surprised the both of us.

"Of course," I breathed. "You can kiss me anytime."

He smiled slightly, and then leaned in to kiss my lips gently. He continued to cradle my face with his hands. He slowly backed away, looking at me with a mysterious look on his face.

Finally, he dropped his hands.

"I don't remember you," he said, honestly.

I started sobbing again. I felt so hopeless.

"But, I believe you," he added.

I looked up, shocked.

"You do?!" I couldn't believe my ears.

"There's something familiar about you," he said. "And when I kissed you, I felt like maybe it wasn't the first time."

"It wasn't," I insisted. More like the *thousandth* time.

"In fact, when I first saw you standing on the deck, I had this feeling that I knew you. It was odd. I hadn't ever met you, but you didn't seem like a stranger either," he clarified.

I nodded, trying to encourage him to remember.

But it was no use. While Benjamin felt a familiarity around me, he didn't remember anything about our time together. How I wish I could make him remember..

But I knew this was the best way. Benjamin was no longer cursed - he was free to live and leave his ship without feeling an ounce of pain. And even though we'd had to start our relationship from scratch, we were able to be together now. We could build a life together - on the shore. Though it hurt tremendously that our memories were gone from this reality, they weren't *really* gone. They could *never* be gone from my heart. And there they'd always stay, all of my favorite memories... the first time we kissed, the time he made me a romantic dinner that we enjoyed underneath the stars. I would cherish them forever. In fact, I was determined not to forget them; so I started writing them down in a journal. Benjamin would never understand everything I'd gone through to be with him, but it was all worth it.

Chapter 17: All I Ever Really Wanted

"Claire?" he called to me. His voice brought instant calm to my soul. "Would you like some tea?" He pushed open his bedroom door, where I was sitting on his bed, writing in my journal. It had become a favorite pastime of mine.

"Yes, please," I told him. He brought me a hot cup and sat down on the bed next to me.

Benjamin and I had spent a lot of time together since I finally made my way back to him. It had been about two weeks since that day. I'd spend my days writing my favorite memories of us in my journal, and in the evenings, he'd come sit next to me and ask me to read them aloud. Every now and then, I would pause to gauge his reaction. He was usually smiling. I was happy to share our memories, and still hopeful that someday, somehow he would remember the special times we had.

"What did you write about today?" he asked, genuinely curious.

Today's entry was tough to think about. It wasn't necessarily a happy memory, but it was one I didn't want to forget, nonetheless.

"I wrote about the time that you left your ship to rescue me, when I was taken by another crew," I told him. I remembered the pain he felt that day, and how weak and ill he became afterwards.

"It was after that when I first told you I loved you," I said. He grabbed my hand, smiling sweetly.

Benjamin had not kissed me since that first day. He allowed me to sleep in his bedroom, probably because I insisted. He always slept on the floor. It turns out, Benjamin is a complete gentleman no matter which timeline he's on. But he'd sit next to me on the bed every evening and listen to our memories. He actually seemed very eager to hear about them.

"You're a gifted storyteller, you know," he told me one night. I sighed. I wasn't telling *stories*. I was telling the truth about what really happened. Granted, it was in a different timeline that he never actually experienced so he had no recollection. But, still.

"I wish you didn't think they were just stories," I replied. "These are so much more than that. These are all of our memories." I closed the journal and held it close to my heart. I felt my eyes start to well up with tears.

"I love when you read them to me," Benjamin replied sweetly. He put his hand under my chin and lifted my face slightly. A single tear rolled down my cheek. The chemistry between the two of us was undeniable. Even Benjamin couldn't deny it. I was hopeful that we'd someday, somehow get back to where we'd left off: *in love.*

I reached up to grab his hand. I pulled it away from my face, and held it in my lap. I played with his fingers.

"Perhaps we should make more memories, Claire," he whispered. I smiled back at him.

"I would love that," I responded.

He leaned in slowly to kiss me, but this time, it wasn't gentle. It was with a passion that I remembered vividly; one that I longed to stay forever.

I kissed him back with as much passion as I could muster. Soon, my journal was on the floor and my hands were in his hair.

After a few minutes, he pulled away slowly.

"Did we used to kiss like that often?" he wondered, looking at me curiously.

"All the time," I assured him, grinning. He smiled.

"Will that one make your journal?" He asked, teasingly.

I laughed. "Definitely."

He chuckled.

"I'm looking forward to making many more memories with you, Claire Walker," he said, cradling my face with both hands.

I could feel my heart skipping beats inside my chest. I felt happy. Was everything perfect? Not exactly. There was so much that Benjamin didn't know; that he'd never experienced in this life. There were things that he would never get the chance to experience again. And I *had* experienced those things - it was the very reason why I loved him the way that I did.

But if I learned anything from this whole experience, it was that life wasn't perfect. There's choices to be made, plans get ruined, and people get hurt. I had fallen in love with a pirate living in the 1800s. He was cursed, but I was determined to be with him no matter what. Maybe my plan didn't work out perfectly, but at least I ended up with Benjamin. I could only move forward now. I *would* move forward now.

"That's all I ever really wanted," I replied.